BIG BUILDERS

by **Susan Korman**

illustrated by **Joel Snyder**

D1613612

Boom! Boom!
One morning a loud noise woke up Jack.
"Get up quick, Jack," cried his brother, Robbie. "There are some big builders outside!"

Jack jumped out of bed and ran to the window.
Dozens of trees in the woods had been knocked down.
Now a yellow bulldozer was clearing away the stumps.
Jack saw some other big trucks, too.

"It's a construction site," Jack said. "Let's go see what they're building."

Jack and Robbie got dressed quickly and raced across their backyard toward the woods.

Jack liked watching the bulldozer's big caterpillar tracks roll across the ground. Its blade pushed away dirt, rocks, and trees.

"Good morning, boys!" The driver waved to Jack and Robbie. Jack waved back. "What are you building?" he called.

"Some new houses," the driver said. "Soon you'll have new neighbors."

It will be fun to have new neighbors, Jack thought.

But he loved to play in the woods. Sometimes he and
Robbie played hide-and-seek. On other days, they found long,
pointy sticks and turned them into swords. Jack's favorite spot
was the old oak tree. Everyday he climbed the tree and looked
out at the view. Then he swung down through the branches,
just like Tarzan swinging through the jungle.

As Jack watched the bulldozer, he felt sad. Where am I
going to play now? he wondered.

Just then Robbie waved Jack over. "Come here, Jack!" he called.

Robbie was watching the backhoe's big bucket scoop up dirt. Jack hurried over. "What's it digging?" he asked.

"A trench," someone else answered.

Surprised, Jack turned around.
A construction worker in a hard hat was watching the backhoe, too.

"The backhoe's bucket digs trenches for pipes," she explained. "Then, after the pipes are laid in the ground, the backhoe's shovel will push the dirt back over them."

"Wow," Jack said. He didn't know that a backhoe did two jobs.

The construction worker's name was Rosa.

"It's not safe to explore a construction site without a grownup," Rosa told them. "Would you like me to give you a special tour?"

"Yes!" Jack and Robbie said at once.

Rosa went into the trailer and came out with two hard hats. "Here you go," she said, smiling.

Jack put on his hard hat. So did Robbie. Jack thought they looked like real construction workers now!

Rosa showed them a cement mixer.

Chung! Chung! Chung!

The cement mixer's barrel turned round and round.

Rosa told Jack and Robbie that the cement mixer was mixing concrete for the houses' foundations.

"After the concrete is poured into the ground," she explained "the workers can start building the frames for the houses."

Jack noticed another truck dragging a blade along the ground. "What does that truck do?" he asked Rosa.

"It's a grader," Rosa said. "Its job is to—"

"I know!" Robbie said. "The grader helps to build roads by making the roadbed smooth."

Rosa nodded. "That's right, Robbie," she said. Then she pointed to another truck. "Here comes the dump truck with a

load of rocks. The rocks will be used to fill in the holes before the road gets paved."

Jack watched the dump truck lift its big dumper. There was a loud noise and a cloud of dust as the rocks poured onto the ground.

The dump truck driver let Jack and Robbie climb into the cab. He showed them how to push the lever that controlled the dumper in the back of the truck.

After the boys jumped down from the big truck, Jack took off his hard hat and held it out to Rosa.

"Thank you for showing us all the big builders at the construction site, Rosa," he said.

"You're welcome, Jack," Rosa answered. Her brown eyes twinkled. "But our tour's not over yet. Come along with me. I want to show you one more thing."

Jack and Robbie hurried to keep up as Rosa raced across the construction site. Where is Rosa taking us? Jack wondered.

He'd thought that she'd already shown them all the big builders.
t last Rosa stopped. "Here we are," she called out.

As Jack gazed around, he felt sad again. His favorite tree was still here, but the rest of the trees in this spot had been cleared away.

"Rosa, why did you bring us here?" Robbie asked.

Rosa's smile grew wider. "I wanted to show you *your* construction site," she said.

"I don't understand, Rosa," Jack said.

"We're going to build a playground here," Rosa explained. She unfolded a big sheet of paper. "This is the blueprint for the new playground. Soon you and your family, and your neighbors, can help to build it."

"Jack! Robbie!" Their father called one morning. "Connor and Annie are here!"

Jack and Robbie put on their hard hats and raced downstairs. They were going back to the construction site with their new friends. Today was the day that they had been waiting for. They were going to build a new playground!

Jack and Connor built a jungle gym with Jack's father. Robbie and Annie helped Rosa and Jack's mom make a fort. Lots of neighbors pitched in to put together slides and monkey bars, even a moving bridge!

Jack climbed up into the oak tree. He looked down at the new playground. The woods were gone, but he had helped to build a new place to play.

And it had been his idea to hang a rope swing from the oak tree's thickest branch. Now everyone in the neighborhood could swing from the tree, just like Tarzan swinging through the jungle.

Jack smiled proudly. Today he was a big builder too!